Meet
Snugglepot and Cuddlepie

Gumnut Babies™

A Scholastic Australia book

In the big gumtrees live the little gumnut babies.
Snugglepot and Cuddlepie lived with their family
among the leaves of the very tallest gum tree.

One day, their friend Mrs Kookaburra came to visit.

'Tell us a story!' Cuddlepie begged.

'Tell us about humans!' dared Snugglepot.

Mrs Kookaburra leant in close and began her yarn. 'Humans are as strong as the wind, swift as the river, fierce as the sun. Humans are taller than the biggest branch on the biggest gum tree in all the land.'

The younger nuts gasped and huddled in closer.

'I want to see a human!' said Snugglepot.

'But what if humans are as bad as bad?' said Cuddlepie.

'We don't know what we might find.'

'That's what makes it so exciting!' said Snugglepot.

Cuddlepie seemed unsure.

Before dawn, when everyone was still asleep,
Snugglepot and Cuddlepie crept out of bed . . .

They were off to find a human.

The road was hot and dusty as the two small gumnuts walked further than they ever had before.

'Where are you going?' asked a big lizard,
basking on a rock by the roadside.
'We're going to see humans!' boasted Snugglepot.
'But only in the distance,' added Cuddlepie.
'Can I come too?' asked the friendly lizard.

And so Mr Lizard joined the friends on their adventure.

As the sun travelled across the sky, the friends came upon a marvellous festival. There were nuts and blossoms dancing under glowing lanterns.

One blossom was sitting alone, so Snugglepot asked her to dance.
Ragged Blossom was so happy.

When the next morning came, they prepared to set off once more.

'Where are you going?' Ragged Blossom asked.

'We're going to see humans!' declared Snugglepot.

'But only in the distance,' said Cuddlepie.

'Can I come too?' asked the lonely blossom.

And so the four new friends continued on their way.

The friends stopped to rest, when out of the bushes they heard a faint voice calling, 'Help me! Help me!'

They ran towards the sound.

The four friends discovered a terrible thing. A baby possum was caught in a steel cage, crying for help.

'Who did this to you?' asked Mr Lizard.

'Humans,' whimpered the possum.

'What can we do?' asked Ragged Blossom.

Just then a great noise sounded on the breeze.

'Humans! Humans!' Cuddlepie cried.

The friends hid.

'It's a giant,' murmured Snugglepot as he peered over a branch.

'It looks like us!' marvelled Cuddlepie.

'Rotten traps!' the human said.

'Don't worry little possum, I'll get you out.'

Snugglepot and Cuddlepie looked
on curiously as the human gently
released the possum.

'I wonder if all humans are kind to bush creatures like that?' said Cuddlepie, as Mr Lizard helped the frightened possum.

'I hope so,' said Ragged Blossom.

The possum thanked the friends and went on his way.

'Hurrah! We have seen a human,' said Snugglepot.
'But only in the distance,' added Cuddlepie.
'What shall we do next?' asked Snugglepot,
as they walked on into the bush.

And so began the adventures of Snugglepot and Cuddlepie.